The Cow That Got Her Wish

by Margaret Hillert

Illustrated by Krystyna Stasiak

DEAR CAREGIVER, The *Beginning-to-Read* series is a carefully written collection of classic readers you may remember from your own childhood. Each book features text comprised of common sight words to provide your child ample practice reading the words that appear most frequently in written text. The many additional details in the pictures enhance the story and offer the opportunity for you to help your child expand oral language and develop comprehension.

Begin by reading the story to your child, followed by letting him or her read familiar words and soon your child will be able to read the story independently. At each step of the way, be sure to praise your reader's efforts to build his or her confidence as an independent reader. Discuss the pictures and encourage your child to make connections between the story and his or her own life. At the end of the story, you will find reading activities and a word list that will help your child practice and strengthen beginning reading skills.

Above all, the most important part of the reading experience is to have fun and enjoy it!

Shannon Cannon

Shannon Cannon,
Literacy Consultant

Norwood House Press • P.O. Box 316598 • Chicago, Illinois 60631
For more information about Norwood House Press please visit our website at *www.norwoodhousepress.com* or call 866-565-2900.

LIBRARY OF CONGRESS CATALOGING-IN-PUBLICATION DATA
Hillert, Margaret.
  The cow that got her wish / Margaret Hillert ; illustrated by Krystyna Stasiak. — Rev. and expanded library ed.
    p. cm. — (Beginning-to-read series)
  Summary: Brownie the cow tries very hard to jump over the moon.
  ISBN-13: 978-1-59953-189-2 (library edition : alk. paper)
  ISBN-10: 1-59953-189-5 (library edition : alk. paper) [1. Stories in rhyme. 2. Cows—Fiction.] I. Stasiak, Krystyna, ill. II. Title.
  PZ8.3.H554Cp 2008
  [E]—dc22   2008001663

Beginning-to-Read series (c) 2009 by Margaret Hillert.
Library edition published by permission of Pearson Education, Inc. in arrangement with Norwood House Press, Inc. All rights reserved.
This book was originally published by Follett Publishing Company in 1981.

"I want to have fun,"
said Brownie, the cow.
"I want to have fun—
and I think I know how.

"There once was a cow
that jumped over the moon.
That's what I want to do,
and I'll start right at noon."

"Why, I can't play the fiddle.
I can't play a tune.
And a silly old cow
can't jump over the moon."

"Oh, no," said her friends.
"If you try such a jump,
do you know what will happen?
You're sure to go BUMP.

"And besides," they all said,
"you can't do it at noon!
Way up in the sky
you can't see any moon."

The cow was not happy.
She ate and she sat.
She sat and she ate
and she waited and sat.

"I'll wait till the sun sets,
and then very soon,
I know I'll be up, up,
and over the moon.

"I will go for a walk.

"I will climb up a hill
and jump over the moon.
Yes, I will. Yes, I will.

11

"I think I can make it.
Just look at me jump.
One, two, three. Here I go.
I go up, up, and —

BUMP!"

"Now, look," said her friends.
"Here's a lump and a hump.
What a silly old Brownie
to think you can jump."

"But I want to, I want to,
I want to, I say.
I know I can do it.
I'll find a good way.

"I'm tired," said Brownie.
"I sit and I sit.
I never have fun.
Not a bit. Not a bit.

"I know what I'll do.
I will try a balloon.
I'm sure that will help me
jump over the moon.

"A big, big balloon
is the thing that I need
to get over the moon.
Yes, indeed. Yes, indeed.

"Up, up, I will go now.
Up, up, I will jump.
This balloon is a help.
Here I go. Here I —

BUMP!"

A little raccoon
who sat on a stump
said, "I'll help you.
I'll help you
to make that big jump.

23

"Just look over here.
Do you see what I see?
Here's the moon
round and yellow
and big as can be.

"If you take a big run,
if you make a big jump,
you'll go over the moon,
and you will not go BUMP."

So the brown and white cow
took a run and a jump.
And she made it! She made it
without any BUMP.

"I did it!
I did it!
Oh, thank you, Raccoon,
for now I'm the cow
that jumped over the moon."

The following activities support the findings of the National Reading Panel that determined the most effective components for reading instruction are: Phonemic Awareness, Phonics, Vocabulary, Fluency, and Text Comprehension.

Phonemic Awareness: The diphthong /ou/ sound

Oral Blending: Say the sounds of the following words separately and ask your child to listen to the sounds and say the whole word:

/k/ + /ou/ = cow   /n/+ /ou/ = now

/h/+ /ou/ = how   /h/ + /ou/ + /l/ = howl

/d/+ /ou/ + n = down   /gr/+ /ou/ + l = growl

/b/+ /ou/ = bow   /b/r + /ou/ + /n/ = brown

/cl/ + /ou/ + n = clown   /pl/+ /ou/ = plow

/t/ + ou/ + /n/ = town   /ch/ + /ou/ = chow

Phonics: The letters o and w

1. Demonstrate how to form the letters **o** and **w** for your child.

2. Have your child practice writing **o** and **w** at least three times each.

3. Write down the following words and ask your child to underline the letters **ow** in each word:

cow	Brownie	now	how	plow
brown	howl	growl	bow	down
chow	town	vow	crown	scowl

Vocabulary: Day and Night

1. Write the words **Daytime** and **Nighttime** on two pieces of paper.

2. Ask your child to draw pictures of several things he or she does at night and during the day on each paper.

3. Label each picture. Read each label and ask your child to repeat it.

4. Ask your child to read each label.

5. Give your child a clue about each picture, without using its name, and ask your child to point to the correct picture/label.

Fluency: Shared Reading

1. Reread the story to your child at least two more times while your child tracks the print by running a finger under the words as they are read. Ask your child to read the words he or she knows with you.

2. Reread the story taking turns, alternating readers between sentences or pages.

Text Comprehension: Discussion Time

1. Ask your child to retell the sequence of events in the story.

2. To check comprehension, ask your child the following questions:

   • Is this story real? How do you know?

   • Why did the cow have trouble jumping over the moon?

   • How did the raccoon help Brownie jump over the moon?

   • Think of something you had trouble doing by yourself. Who helped you, and how did they help you?

WORD LIST

The Cow that Got Her Wish uses the 124 words listed below.

12 words serve as an introduction to new vocabulary while 112 words are pre-primer. This list can be used to practice reading the words that appear in the text. You may wish to write the words on index cards and use them to help your child build automatic word recognition. Regular practice with these words will enhance your child's fluency in reading connected text.

Pre-Primer Words   **New Vocabulary Words**

a	get	little	say	to	besides
all	go	look	see	took	
and	good	lump	sets	try	climb
any			she	two	
at	happy	made	silly		fiddle
ate	have	make	sit	up	
	help	me	sky		happen
balloon	her		so	very	
be	here('s)	need	soon		indeed
big	hill	never	start	walk	
bit	how	no	such	want	moon
brown	hump	not	sun	was	
Brownie		now	sure	way	noon
bump	I			what	
but	I'll	oh	take	white	once
	I'm	old	thank	who	
can	if	on	that('s)	why	raccoon
can't	in	one	the	will	round
cow	is	over	then	without	
	it		there		stump
did		play	they	yellow	
do	jump(ed)		thing	yes	tune
	just	right	think	you	
find		run	this	you'll	
for	know		three	you're	
friends		said	till		
fun		sat	tired		

ABOUT THE AUTHOR Margaret Hillert has written over 80 books for children who are just learning to read. Her books have been translated into many different languages and over a million children throughout the world have read her books. She first started writing poetry as a child and has continued to write for children and adults throughout her life. A first grade teacher for 34 years, Margaret is now retired from teaching and lives in Michigan where she likes to write, take walks in the morning, and care for her three cats.

Photograph by Glenna Washburn

ABOUT THE ADVISER Shannon Cannon contributed the activities pages that appear in this book. Shannon serves as a literacy consultant and provides staff development to help improve reading instruction. She is a frequent presenter at educational conferences and workshops. Prior to this she worked as an elementary school teacher and as president of a curriculum publishing company.